FOREWORD

Welcome, Reader!

Here at Young Writers our aim is to encourage creativity in children and to inspire a love of the written word. Each competition we create is tailored to the relevant age group, hopefully giving each child the inspiration and incentive to create their own piece of work, whether it's a poem or a short story. We truly believe that seeing their work in print gives pupils a sense of achievement and pride.

For Young Writers' latest nationwide competition, Spooky Sagas, we gave primary school pupils the task of tackling one of the oldest story-telling traditions: the ghost story. However, we added a twist – they had to write it as a mini saga, a story in just 100 words!

These pupils rose to the challenge magnificently and this resulting collection of spooky sagas will certainly give you the creeps! You may meet friendly ghosts or creepy clowns, or be taken on Halloween adventures to haunted mansions and ghostly graveyards!

So if you think you're ready... read on.

SPOOKY SAGAS

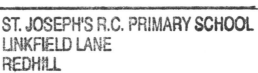

ST. JOSEPH'S R.C. PRIMARY SCHOOL
LINKFIELD LANE
REDHILL
SURREY, RH1 1DU

SURREY & SUSSEX

Edited By Jess Giaffreda

First published in Great Britain in 2019 by:

 Young**Writers**

Young Writers
Remus House
Coltsfoot Drive
Peterborough
PE2 9BF
Telephone: 01733 890066
Website: www.youngwriters.co.uk

CONTENTS

Gonville Academy, Croydon

Denise Koudou (10) — 1
Adam Craigen (10) — 2

Gorringe Park Primary School, Mitcham

Sankari Archer (11) — 3
Aaliyah Kabous (11) — 4
Zahra Asif (11) — 5
Thaanujan Sivagananthan (11) — 6
Kajan Jeyaramachandran (11) — 7
Shyla Stirling-Sowden (10) — 8
Kassidy Nyunt-Gomes (11) — 9
Jakub Swilpa (11) — 10
Akshika Thuraurajasingam (10) — 11
Sulayman Kiyani (11) — 12
Mark Rosko (10) — 13
Abbinaya Viknesh (10) — 14
Leo Huie (10) — 15
Afraz Hussain (11) — 16
Alex Green (10) — 17
Divyan Senthuran (9) — 18
Suraiya Rahman (10) — 19
Asha Monplaisir (11) — 20
Caitlin Alice Buckley (10) — 21
Maya Farrow (10) — 22
Amber Hughes (11) — 23
Narmada Selvanathan (9) — 24
Matilda Widdicombe (10) — 25
Shivasri Kathiresan (11) — 26
Keziah Adomah (9) — 27
Amaya Hill (11) — 28
Ali Abatiou (11) — 29
Darcy Elizabeth Jones (10) — 30

Jessica Rogerson (10) — 31
Hannah Abdulkadir Habad (11) — 32
Connor Spencer-Jackson (11) — 33
Evanam Kpodo (9) — 34
Tolu Oluwole (11) — 35
Kristian Alleyne Xavier Cornwall Baptiste (9) — 36
Edvin Sujkovic (10) — 37
Morgan Craib (10) — 38
Yousaf Rahail Afzal (10) — 39
Amelia Kolodziejczyk (7) — 40
Kacper Maliszewski (11) — 41
Manli Elihu Kpakoe Addo (11) — 42
Kayla Spellen (10) — 43
Shanthose Vasanthakumar (10) — 44
Ruslan Konopackis (10) — 45
Jadusha Ramesh (11) — 46
Sophie Collins (10) — 47
Ricardo Ferreira (10) — 48
Lena Kedzia (9) — 49
Rayan Moussaif (10) — 50
Julia Kalisz (10) — 51
Vivian Doan (10) — 52
Yassar Muhammad Farooq (10) — 53
Alan Lak (8) — 54
Dominika Boraczynska (9) — 55
Kieran (11) — 56
Taiyon Harper-Fuller (7) — 57
Wilma Sanyanga (10) — 58
Bhavini Vimalan (9) — 59
Rio Cole (10) — 60
Annaliese St Louis (7) — 61
Roman Miri (9) — 62

Great Ballard School, Chichester

Hayden Terry (10)	63
Ella Wakefield (9)	64
Olivia Cook (9)	65
Charlotte Hayesmore (10)	66
Lottie-Rose Best (9)	67

Heene CE Primary School, Worthing

Daisy Amelia Mundy (10)	68
Aditya Vasisht (7)	69
Charlie James Fox (10)	70

Jessie Younghusband Primary School, Chichester

Iona Sherwood (8)	71
Isabelle Coton (8)	72
Noah Baverstock (8)	73
Ava Lily Harman (9)	74
Daisy Dearing (8)	75
Rosa Brown (8)	76
Olive Kus (8)	77

Meridian Primary School, Peacehaven

Nikki Toth (10)	78
Mollie Haselup (9)	79
Marissa Hollie Palmer (10)	80
Michalina Fielek (10)	81
Elizabeth Shalonina (9)	82
Anya Davis (9)	83
Ruby Roberts (10)	84
Luna Saulyte (10)	85
Isabelle Raggett (10)	86
Faith Vickery (9)	87
Lilly Knapikova (9)	88
Olivia Julie Coughtrey (9)	89

Peasmarsh CE Primary School, Peasmarsh

Abby Tittle (11)	90
Nial Wilde (10)	91

St Joseph's Catholic Primary School, Haywards Heath

Oliver Skinner (9)	92
Joshua Foy (10)	93
Emma Grace Rochford (10)	94
Brooke Bashford-Dickens (10)	95
Daisy Belle Stoodley Leppard (10)	96
Emily Daisy Hilton (9)	97
Katie Rochford (8)	98
Aglaïa Carvalho-Dubost (10)	99
Chelsy Mae Dupiano (10)	100
Alex Ladd (9)	101
Elsie Tibble (9)	102

St Joseph's Catholic Primary School, Redhill

Genevieve McArdell (10)	103
Leigh Steadman (10)	104
Florence Moore (9)	105
Isla Mehta (9)	106
Isaac Blackburn (9)	107
Sophie Pither (9)	108
Charlie Rocco Knap (9)	109
Joshua Jupp (10)	110

Stafford Junior School, Eastbourne

Mollie Ann Bradley (8)	111
Charlotte Smeeton (7)	112

The Globe Primary Academy, Lancing

Natasha Zoe Downes (9)	113
Nathaniel Dene (9)	114

Harry Waddup (9)	115
Zachary Manser (9)	116
Yolanda Isabel Thomas Negro (10)	117
Charlie Nettlefold (9)	118
Jack David Standen (10)	119
Indiana Bazeley (10)	120
Jorge Sexton (10)	121
Olivia Marsh (9)	122
Megan Clarke (10)	123
Libby Bedford (9)	124
Elliot Braiden (10)	125
Olivia Lockwood (10)	126
Layla Pelton (10)	127
Sidney Ager (10)	128
Oliver Snuggs-Lee (9)	129
Mimi Raynsford (10)	130
Chloe Brisley (9)	131
Evie Hilton (10)	132
Ella Croome (9)	133
Bethany Hall (10)	134
Ruby Heywood (10)	135
Chloe Douglass (10)	136
Faye Walls (9)	137
Matthew Floate (10)	138
Adam Hacker (9)	139
Erin Atkinson (10)	140
Lewis Sharman (10)	141
Liam Floate (10)	142
Grace Harris (10)	143
Jorja-Carol Harris (9)	144
Demi Leigh Leggett (9)	145
Lily Green (10)	146
Lily Hollingdale (9)	147
Isla Riley (9)	148
Brooke Dixon (9)	149
Ebonii Humphrey (9)	150
Kara Price (9)	151
Darsh Khadka (9)	152

The Towers Convent School, Upper Beeding

Eve Baker (10)	153
Amelia Birse (9)	154
Kitty Rayner (9)	155
Sophia Nicholls (9)	156

West Rise Junior School, Eastbourne

Megan Robins (9)	157
Mitch Morgan (9)	158
Amelia Gurr (9)	159
Stefania Turcu (10)	160
Eve Isobel Van Der Geyten (10)	161
Louie Emo (9)	162

THE
SPOOKY
SAGAS

THE GOBLIN

In a cave was a grotesque goblin staring into the darkness with its bloodshot red eye shining in the moonlight. Sophie, a little girl, meandered into the forest, searching for a place to trick or treat. She glared at her surroundings, anxious of her every step.
Back in the cave, the goblin had disguised himself as a human. Suddenly, Sophie felt something dig into the skin of her arm. The last thing she saw was a shadow darting across the circumference of the forest. Sophie lay there, bound hands and feet. She was never seen again...

Denise Koudou (10)
Gonville Academy, Croydon

A HALLOWEEN WORTH DYING FOR!

I stood there, endlessly giving out sweets at my doorstep. Finally, I had an empty bowl in my hand.

When I stepped inside, there were huge stains of scarlet blood dripping down the wall. I called my brother. Then I heard a knock at the windows. There were zombies clawing at them and I knew I was in for big trouble! Full of adrenaline, I saw my brother in the gang as the glass shattered. The zombies raced at me as my brother tore at my T-shirt...

Adam Craigen (10)
Gonville Academy, Croydon

JUST A GAME

They were running, running through the forest with the wind brushing their cheeks. Jessica's heart thumped. Trembling with anxiety, Jessica had secretly escaped in the night. She couldn't hear her friends.

"Hello?" she yelled.

Why did she go? She sat down and began massaging her ankle.

"Over here!" spluttered a voice.

"Here, we should play!"

There was an isolated house. Jessica shuddered...

"Come on, show yourself you're not a wimp!"

They went in the house. Jessica found a room with dolls, dolls with knives chanting.

"Come play with me!" a piercing scream echoed.

A hand touched her. She was gone...

Sankari Archer (11)

Gorringe Park Primary School, Mitcham

THE WATCHER

I need to find where my brother has disappeared. He was last seen in the abandoned church down my road. I opened the creaky door to an everlasting hallway. At the end of the corridor, there was a cross. The door shut and locked. I was trapped! Suddenly, a text popped on my phone. It was by '???'
"Hello, Alex."
"Who are you?" I asked.
"I'm The Watcher. I know where your brother is..." The Watcher replied, "I'll show you."
Then an apparition appeared out of thin air.
"Now you are mine!"
Demons appeared.
"Goodnight, Alex, sweet dreams."
"Argh!"

Aaliyah Kabous (11)
Gorringe Park Primary School, Mitcham

THE FORBIDDEN SCHOOL...

One spine-chilling day, two teens had a deadly plan to go to the forbidden school, but they didn't know the chances of coming back were not good.

Once they entered, they saw a blinding light switched on.

"What was that?" exclaimed Luna, looking regretfully.

"Should we go look?" cried Lexy, looking paranoid.

"You su-" she bellowed rapidly as another light turned on.

"Here, take these and stand behind me..."

As they took the metal rods, they heard big, eerie footsteps. *Twitch!* The torch turned on. Suddenly, they ran in the sinister room and felt a heavy head...

Zahra Asif (11)
Gorringe Park Primary School, Mitcham

THE ABANDONED PALACE!

We were walking through a spine-chilling graveyard, different sounds were heard and it made Jack shiver so he grabbed onto me.
I said, "Stop being a coward!"
He understood my impatience and carried on with the voyage. Soon we bumped into a colossal building. We looked up to see a half-broken palace.
Jack trembled and whispered, "No, James... let's go back, come on!"
I glared at him and chuckled. I opened the huge door and a world of murkiness shocked me. Behind me, Jack stumbled, his face looking aghast. Suddenly, a belittling shadow took over the entire room, leaving trails...

Thaanujan Sivagananthan (11)
Gorringe Park Primary School, Mitcham

THE BIRTHDAY RETURN

There was a deafening ringing. The ringing petrified anyone who heard it. It was the phone! Henry wearily walked up to it, not knowing who it was.
"Uhh... who is this?"
"Come!"
"Where?"
"Come to the ink machine!"
It was then that the phone fell silent. So he went to the ink machine and everything was fine - *not!* Henry had to hide behind a wall, hoping Bendy, the clown, Sammy and Ugandan Knuckles wouldn't find him. Henry ran to the side of a wall and saw cake. Then he turned around and saw his friends singing 'Happy Birthday' cheerfully.

Kajan Jeyaramachandran (11)
Gorringe Park Primary School, Mitcham

THE WORST HALLOWEEN

One spooky, dark Halloween afternoon, Aliza was walking home from the market when she came across a blood-dripping strange boulder that said: 'Free candy, this way!'

Well, that's what she thought it said. She happily ran straight through the alley that the boulder was pointing at and knocked it down. What she didn't know was that it didn't say: 'Free candy, this way!' it said: 'Danger! No free candy this way!'

"Arghhh!" screamed a voice.

Now Aliza had been gone for a whole day. Her family were worried. What they didn't know was that Aliza was dead.

Shyla Stirling-Sowden (10)
Gorringe Park Primary School, Mitcham

THE TRUTH OF ALL DARES

Christine's scarlet eyes sat upon Drake's pale face as she drove the sharpened knife through his neck. His lifeless body collapsed as blood spilt onto the cold floor. Dove and Max shot up and backed towards the wall.

"P-please... spare us our lives!" Dove and Max pleaded but Christine was far from controllable. She stepped closer to Dove laughing with cold glinting eyes. The knife found itself in Dove's forehead. Blood was a craze, it was everywhere... Christine pulled the knife out, watching the body fall. She then stabbed Max in the stomach. Watch out... Christine may come for you...

Kassidy Nyunt-Gomes (11)
Gorringe Park Primary School, Mitcham

JASON'S REVENGE

One dark, misty night, campers were telling stories when one camper went missing. They went to the hut to see if he was there but all they saw was a mask and blood...

"Jason?" Jake said.

"Who is he?" said Rio.

Jake rushed out the car when the killer was there with a machete. Jake shot Jason and went in the car. Jason screamed as they drove away.

Two minutes later, they heard a noise like, "Help!"

It was Ali, they'd left him behind.

"I thought he was dead!" said Rio.

"Noo!" the voice helplessly yelled again.

Jakub Swilpa (11)
Gorringe Park Primary School, Mitcham

FAMILIAR FACE

Light shone at the dusty window, an isolated house towered in front of me.

As I entered the room, I heard an ear-piercing, shrill scream attack my ears. Looking around, I saw ripped off dolls' heads dripping blood around the room. My mouth dropped immediately. The piano was working on its own, what was lurking in there? *Slam!* The door shut. Why did I come here? I let out a scream but nothing came out. *Tap! Tap!* Suddenly, the floorboard creaked. Somebody approached. I waited eagerly.

"Who is it?" I asked.

A black figure stood. It was familiar...

Akshika Thuraurajasingam (10)

Gorringe Park Primary School, Mitcham

HAUNTED HOSPITAL

After a long, exhausting day at school, Mike was walking home. He walked through the dark, damp forest.

When he reached home, his brother opened the door. They headed out on their way to the abandoned hospital so his friends wouldn't think he was scared. They stood opposite the hospital with steamed windows.

After a while, they pulled out their camera and entered. The lights flickered as they stepped foot inside. The door shut behind them. A soft whisper was heard... A tin rolled across the floor. They immediately ran and found a door. Never seen again, the hospital rusted.

Sulayman Kiyani (11)
Gorringe Park Primary School, Mitcham

ON THE RAILS

I'm finally here! The abandoned train station was before my eyes. The reason I came here was everyone in the town forbade their children to come here - including Mum. *I'll prove that they're all cowards!*
The dull, cobwebbed wall of the train station glared at me. It wasn't scary at all. I decided to stand on the rails just for the fun of it. I laughed. How cowardly the whole town was! Suddenly, a black steam train emerged from the station tunnel. It was rushing straight at me. Suddenly, it stopped... My mini train had run out of coal.

Mark Rosko (10)
Gorringe Park Primary School, Mitcham

THE CLOWN UNDER THE BED

James, an old man, was home alone, or was he? He lay on the sofa when he heard a loud creak. *Creak!* Suddenly, the lights started to flicker. Red blood dripped into his hand. He heard a deafening scream. As quick as a flash, he went to check. A blood-curdling, horrifying clown with a razor-sharp knife was there.
"I'm going to kill you!" it squeaked.
James ran as fast as lightning.
I must be imagining it, he thought. He got ready for bed and went to sleep. Little did he know, the clown was waiting for him under his bed...

Abbinaya Viknesh (10)
Gorringe Park Primary School, Mitcham

THE POISONOUS PRISON

In her cold, dark cell, Georgia Mayfield sat, staring blankly at the dirty, slimy wall. She pictured her nice, cosy home and how she had robbed everything inside it. She wished she could take back the last few days and live them again.

The next gloomy morning, Georgia woke up to the stench of rat and mouse pie. She flopped out of bed and dragged herself to the toilets. In the bathtub, Georgia sat, worrying. Suddenly, a grotesque hand reached for her leg and pulled her slowly under the grimy, smelly water.

"Help!" she cried, but nobody heard her.

Leo Huie (10)

Gorringe Park Primary School, Mitcham

WHO'S THERE?

I walked on the damp grass to find my friend's house. The woods troubled me, for many leaves twitched on the ground. I kept walking until I suddenly saw a shadow.

Finally, I found Tedison's house, but I couldn't find any sign of him. Fear struck through my body like lightning, but just as I was about to leave, a chill shivered down my slender spine... I didn't check the basement. I couldn't see anything until a chair appeared. I knew who it was. Ruby blood trickled down, but before I could open my mouth, something knocked me out cold...

Afraz Hussain (11)
Gorringe Park Primary School, Mitcham

THE MANSION

Far, far away in the depths of space, there was a scientist called Bob who made a time machine and he tested it on five children and a teenager. *Bang! Pow! Zap!* The experiment went all wrong and the children and teenager got teleported to a graveyard. The children turned around and saw a mansion. The teenager was acting strong and bold so they walked out the haunted mansion. As they walked in, music struck into their ears. As they walked upstairs, the children screamed. "Arghh!"
The lights went out and all the children were gone...

Alex Green (10)
Gorringe Park Primary School, Mitcham

THE MAN-EATING MIRROR

As the uproar of thunder and rain bellowed outside, Ligito looked out of the window, waiting for his parents to come. He went downstairs. As he was walking, he swore a slimy claw grabbed him by the shin. He fell. "Arghh!"

He landed flat faced on the floor. The floor was red with blood. Ligito went and got a plaster for his cheek.

Creak! Creak! Ligito went to the bathroom but he realised he had to go back to get the mop to clean the blood.

After that, he went back to the bathroom and looked at the mirror.

"Nom!"

Divyan Senthuran (9)
Gorringe Park Primary School, Mitcham

HAUNTED HOSPITAL

On Halloween, it was Hope's birthday. It was noon now, so Hope and her friends were going trick or treating but really, they were going to a haunted hospital. The girls came downstairs and Hope explained to her mum that they were going trick or treating.

A few hours later, they arrived.

"This is going to be sick!" blurted out Cam. After that, McKeyla picked the lock. They checked everywhere but no creepy things. Suddenly, *crash!* Everyone screamed. They went to check but nothing was there. Then they turned around...

Suraiya Rahman (10)

Gorringe Park Primary School, Mitcham

WHEN THE GHOST CAME ROUND

Alisha loved mysteries and clues to lead her somewhere interesting. One lonely day, Alisha found an old, precious note. It read: 'There's a ghost at a nearby forest'. The forest was abandoned and lonely. There was a cold breath breathing on her. What was it? She made a blood-curdling scream. She was frightened to death! Her head was twisted with too many thoughts about what it could be. Who was carrying her? At that moment, everything stopped. Now she was confused. Was she dreaming or what?
At that moment, Alisha sat up. It was all a dream!

Asha Monplaisir (11)
Gorringe Park Primary School, Mitcham

VANCOSTA THE VAMPIRE

As Sara and I walked into the village, we knew something was wrong.

"Do you like it girls?" asked Mum.

We stayed quiet. It was nearly night so we went to bed. Mum set up our beds. Mine was rainbow-coloured. Sara said mine was as bright as the sun.

The next morning, we woke up and had breakfast. Mum said we could go out. We played in some of the houses, it got a little darker. We went in one last house, it was really dark...

I squealed, "Sara, stop tickling me!"

"Vancosta the vampire!" someone shouted.

Caitlin Alice Buckley (10)

Gorringe Park Primary School, Mitcham

SPOOKY DREAM

In the middle of the most boring English lesson, a group of friends were having trouble listening. The room started to get really dark until they found themselves outside of school. They chose to forget about it and go to the park.

On the way there, the friends saw weird signs on every wall they passed. It started to get really quiet. The only thing they could hear were blood-curdling screams. They ended up in a pitch-black room. They saw a light switch. They turned the light on and found themselves in class being laughed at by their friends.

Maya Farrow (10)
Gorringe Park Primary School, Mitcham

THE COOKIE THIEF

It was a dark night and I sneaked back into school because there were leftover cookies. I went in and I was looking for them. As I found them, the door opened. I said hello but no answer. Suddenly, the cupboard door opened. When I turned around, they were gone and I followed the cookie crumbs and turned on the light. It was my teacher!

I said to her, "What's wrong?"

She said she wanted some cookies.

I said, "I will share them with you!"

In the end, we sat together eating all the cookies until they were gone.

Amber Hughes (11)

Gorringe Park Primary School, Mitcham

GHOST

It was a stormy night when the roars of thunder spread through the gloomy forest. The bloodthirsty wolves howled eagerly for food...
"Where am I?" said Milo as he stomped through the forest.
"Help!" a voice yelled.
Milo ran towards the voice, thinking it would help him. He dashed in the direction the voice came from. A transparent figure that was floating stopped him.
"You helped me by falling into my trap!" the ghost said, beaming.
It sent shivers up his spine. *Clutch!* Milo was gone...

Narmada Selvanathan (9)
Gorringe Park Primary School, Mitcham

MONSTER HOUSE

"He's taken another trike!" Jake reported to his friends, Tabitha and Sam.

They were watching the possessed house that lurked across the road. The house belonged to a frail man whom Jake recently broke the arm of.

"We go tonight!" exclaimed Jake.

He was a man of oath so that evening, they packed water guns, Tabitha with the smallest, Jake with the next and Sam with the next. They crept across the lawn and opened the door.

The shutters in all the windows crept open.

Little did they know, this was the end...

Matilda Widdicombe (10)

Gorringe Park Primary School, Mitcham

MYSTERY ATTACK

Hi, my name is Zoey. I'm a dead seventeen-year-old. This is my dead life story.
I crept down the cold, dark forest, unaware of my surroundings. Eerie noises could be heard from every corner. A gust of chilly wind went up and twisted my spine. Leaves creaked and crumbled into sand. Shadows loomed around, creeping me out. *Creak! Snap!* A tree branch had snapped behind me. Sweat fell down my forehead. Slowly, I looked around... A loud howl fell across me. A murky shadow fell on me. I looked up. A strange outline of a figure...

Shivasri Kathiresan (11)
Gorringe Park Primary School, Mitcham

THE CREEPY DOLL

At 3am, the witching hour, a gloomy cloud hovered over my new house that was in the heart of the woods. The roars of thunder came rolling down.

I woke up. All of a sudden, I heard a strange voice singing a lullaby. I decided to investigate the house. Then the singing came again. The thunder bashed into the ground one second and the next, I felt something clutch my leg! I looked down only to see a doll with clown make-up!

"Will you play with me?" it said.

A few seconds later, it said. "Oh... *die!*"

Keziah Adomah (9)
Gorringe Park Primary School, Mitcham

erWriters

THE RED BALLOON

Eeek! The door went as it slowly opened. Violet stepped one foot into the abandoned house and looked around but the room was empty. *Pop!* Violet looked left and right but there was nothing there. When Violet looked in front of her, there was a red balloon. She looked up and there was a little boy then he disappeared. Violet followed the balloon to a red room, there was a boy in a cage and he was holding a knife and a balloon.

Then he said, "Come play with some dangerous knives!" He chucked one at her...

Amaya Hill (11)
Gorringe Park Primary School, Mitcham

28

FRIDAY 13TH

One stormy night, a group of campers were camping and telling scary stories. As they turned around, they found a friend with a razor-sharp, spine-chilling machete in his head. They started screaming and shouting, the group started running. It was Jason!
They grabbed a pistol and started shooting him. He didn't die. Jason grabbed a camper and snapped his mouth open. Jason cut a camper's throat and they ran. Jason tried to finish them all. They called a police officer to escape. Three escaped with a police officer, three died.

Ali Abatiou (11)
Gorringe Park Primary School, Mitcham

EMPTY...

My name is Emily. I am lost and need to get home. I'm ten and currently in the middle of a small forest, living in a little cabin. I keep on seeing weird shadows and hearing whispering voices. I'm so petrified! Sadly, I got lost after trick or treating. I feel so lonely and scared. As I go to sleep, something touches my shoulder and once again, I can hear weird voices. I need to get out of this Hell! This place is eerie and unnerving. I walk straight. The twigs crunch underneath me. My poor house... it is completely empty.

Darcy Elizabeth Jones (10)
Gorringe Park Primary School, Mitcham

PERILOUS PLAY DATE

Our teeth chattered and the crisp air engulfed us.

Finally, we'd reached the mansion. We rang the bell and Max opened the door, looking pale. We stepped in and gazed at the hall that looked endless. Then Hayley and I followed Max. Suddenly, he entered a room! We were left perplexed so we walked around to find him. Both of us trailed up a spiral stairway and ended up in a cobweb-filled chamber. We stared around the room. I grabbed a rake and Hayley found torches. We crept around until... *bash!* We were knocked out...

Jessica Rogerson (10)
Gorringe Park Primary School, Mitcham

THE ANCESTORS' CURSE

As the roaring thunder flashed along the sky, there was an unknown sound coming from the attic. The girl slowly went to the cupboard in the attic and stepped inside. The door had shut on her and she couldn't find a way to get out. A flying book flew onto her hand and it had blood dripping from it. The blood went on her hand and her eyes popped out as she screamed.

"Arghh!"

The girl had been cursed! The blood came from her ancestors as it was their house, the house where she was going to be trapped forever...

Hannah Abdulkadir Habad (11)

Gorringe Park Primary School, Mitcham

MICHAEL THE LIVING DUMMY

As I thrashed my arms around, I felt myself getting lightheaded and nauseous. My friends had turned and fled, leaving me to drown. Everything went black. I opened my eyes and couldn't taste anything. I had somehow got into a cupboard of their house. I didn't know what made me do it but I clicked my fingers. I ended up over their sleeping bags. They awoke. "Arghhh!" screamed Emily.

They stared at me as if I was a stranger. I ran to the mirror and saw a dummy staring back. "I am a... a monster!"

Connor Spencer-Jackson (11)

Gorringe Park Primary School, Mitcham

THE HOUSE OF HORRORS

At 1am, the witching hour, thunder and lightning were the only thing you could hear in the eerie, frightening forest. If you went all the way to the end of the forest, you would see an abandoned funfair. In that funfair, there was a house of horrors and living in that house was the evil sorceress. Once, a child went into the house of horrors and was never seen again! The fiendish sorceress used her magic to make all the creatures come out so they'd do the work.

When they were finished with her, she was never seen again...

Evanam Kpodo (9)
Gorringe Park Primary School, Mitcham

THE BOY OF THE GRAVEYARD

My arms were covered in goosebumps. I regretted choosing to cut through the graveyard. Why did I need to sneak out to see my friend anyway? I couldn't back out now. I was too deep in.

I looked around me with the drab, grey gravestones. Then I saw a small body coming towards me from out of the mist. My blood curdled. Then I realised it was just a boy. The boy ran up to me.

"Help me find my parents!"

Then he dragged me underneath a grave. Trapped, I screamed deafeningly and loudly. Then I saw a light...

Tolu Oluwole (11)
Gorringe Park Primary School, Mitcham

THE HOUSE!

One scary night, Vlad and Witcher passed an abandoned house in the middle of the night. It started to rain but that didn't bother them. Then a huge cloud of thunder and lightning hit the house so they went inside.

The door slammed behind them! Vlad and Witcher walked closer, it was dark... Then *Bang!* They both disappeared. They both got sucked up by a vacuum. They found each other in a graveyard and when they looked around, there was a whole bunch of zombies just in front of them! They ran until they died.

Kristian Alleyne Xavier Cornwall Baptiste (9)

Gorringe Park Primary School, Mitcham

THE STUDIO

My name's Slender...Man... erm... Junior. It is a dark night and I am walking home by myself! Then I s-see something m-moving! As I approach, I see the person is quickly running away! Then I see the person stop.
"Arghh!" I screech, then I find myself and Alice in this studio and Alice is also my friend's sister. Then I look behind me and see a sign that says: *Ink Machine!* I turn back around to see a trail of ink... to a door that is locked! Then I open it somehow and I see my brother, Bendy!

Edvin Sujkovic (10)
Gorringe Park Primary School, Mitcham

THE SCARY FOREST

In the middle of the oldest, creepiest forest in the world, there was a rickety old haunted house. Surrounding the house were huge, deep pits of zombies. The smell couldn't be described.

A boy named Conner was running through the forest and came across the spooky house. For some odd reason, he was drawn to it like a magnet. He was caught by a crazy witch! "What are you doing here?" the witch cackled. Then she threw him into a pit and watched him become a half zombie. He was never seen again...

Morgan Craib (10)
Gorringe Park Primary School, Mitcham

THE DOOR

One day in the city of Shrewsbury, a malevolent man named Jigsaw went to buy an abandoned house in a forest to lure people in. One week later, Jigsaw caught a girl named Jess. She was only nine. She knew her amazing life was over.

One hour later, she was stuck in a maze but when she looked up, she saw the roof. It was a house. She went exploring around the maze. She ended up at a creaky door. It said: *Do Not Enter...*

Jess was a very curious girl. She went inside... Ten years later, where was she?

Yousaf Rahail Afzal (10)
Gorringe Park Primary School, Mitcham

KILLER MYSTERY

One deep, dark night, a girl was teleported to another world. She thought it was a dream. It wasn't. She was terrified as she heard a noise like someone was killed. "It sounded like my parents!" the girl shouted loudly. She ran towards the room, nothing was there. In the blink of an eye, she saw a knife next to her head. She turned around but... nothing was there! She then found an exit. She ran out as quickly as she could. Suddenly, she saw her house. She went closer and she saw bloody hands everywhere...

Amelia Kolodziejczyk (7)
Gorringe Park Primary School, Mitcham

THE UNSEEN

I was going to visit my mum. I was still depressed after her tragic death. I walked home from school, I always have to go past these woods due to construction going on. When I was walking to the graveyard through the woods, I heard a bunch of twigs to my left crunch. I ran swiftly.

"Help!" I screamed, but I couldn't hear anything.

It was like a void, just me. All alone.

Eventually, I found out I got hit by a branch.

When I arrived there, I froze completely still like a mannequin...

Kacper Maliszewski (11)
Gorringe Park Primary School, Mitcham

THE DOLL

One dark, spooky day, four teenagers decided to spend the night in the woods without knowing the danger they faced. They were all sitting around the campfire, one of them heard a crack and looked around to find a doll standing with an enormous, razor-sharp machete in its hand. With an evil smile, the lethal doll ran at the speed of light and stabbed the fatal knife into their heads. Two days later, the police were on the scene and all they found was a machete and four bodies lying helplessly on the ground...

Manli Elihu Kpakoe Addo (11)

Gorringe Park Primary School, Mitcham

LIGHTS OUT

Things have never been the same since the accident. We moved to a better house in California because a couple of street boys attacked my son on the same road my daughter died. Me and my husband bought a house which we heard was really good. Whilst taking the boxes out of the boot, Jack just stood there, staring at the door like he was possessed. I told him to go inside but he turned around like he was scared or something.
Night came and I was drifting off to sleep when I heard a knife. The lights went out...

Kayla Spellen (10)
Gorringe Park Primary School, Mitcham

THE ABANDONED HOUSE

One dark day, a girl and her dad were having an astonishing time when they got a knock on the door. When they opened the door, there was a man with a letter. When they opened the letter, there was a house on it. It muttered that if they didn't go to that house by eleven, they would die.

They went to the house, but they didn't want to go in. Then when they tried opening the door, they heard a noise. When they went in, they fell down.

"Arghh!"

They were never to be seen again...

Shanthose Vasanthakumar (10)
Gorringe Park Primary School, Mitcham

THE CUPBOARD

One night, I heard a voice talking about some kind of forbidden cupboard so the next night, I sneaked out of bed and began searching all of the cupboards.

When I arrived at the kitchen, I saw this shadowed figure about the same size as me. It was guarding the kitchen. When it saw me, it made this strange noise! Then when it was looking away, I checked all the cupboards and found a box of... chocolates? The figure was... my mum? The strange noises she was making was just her telling me to go back to bed!

Ruslan Konopackis (10)

Gorringe Park Primary School, Mitcham

THE PIZZA OF DOOM!

Barry, a local pizza man, was delivering pizzas when he went to a city where it was shadowy and only one broken cottage stood. *Knock! Knock! Knock!*
"Anyone there?" he called but no one answered.
That's when he saw a pair of eyes staring at him. Frightened, he rampaged to his car and drove off. As he looked back, he saw a creepy girl holding a teddy and giggling. He got out his car and inquired about her. The man replied that the girl and her mother died ten years ago in a fire...

Jadusha Ramesh (11)
Gorringe Park Primary School, Mitcham

THE RIVER

Someone is behind me, I feel scared and feel their hot breath on the back of my neck. Their eyes burn into me and the only thing I can do is find out how dangerous the person is. I am standing by the murky river, the perfect place to be murdered. I have two members of family in the shack. I had come to get a drink of water.

Finally, I find the courage to turn around. The stranger immediately pushes me.

"My brother, what?"

He laughs an evil laugh as I am left to swim frantically for my life.

Sophie Collins (10)

Gorringe Park Primary School, Mitcham

WELCOME TO HELL

In a dark, cold night, me, Andria and Bea were playing truth or dare, when Bea said, "Andria, I dare you to go to the forest with me."
Before I could say a thing, Andria said, "Okay!" like it was a trip to Heaven! I tried to talk her out but she ignored me, so off they went, leaving me open-mouthed, staring at what seemed like a spider's home.
Suddenly, I heard a scream, it sounded like Andria so I ran until I found a multi-coloured vortex. I was in a place like Hell...

Ricardo Ferreira (10)
Gorringe Park Primary School, Mitcham

THE DEPTHS OF THE WOODS

John was taking a walk in the sunny, peaceful woods as a herd of grey hovered over the area. A loud storm followed along. The peaceful wood had transformed into a shadowful warehouse. There were little critters everywhere! John searched in the depths of the woods. There stood an abandoned cabin. John knew it was now or never. He suspiciously opened the door, knowing this could be his last moment alive. There was a mighty beast, eyes as red as fire. John was pinned to the wall by the beast... what now?

Lena Kedzia (9)
Gorringe Park Primary School, Mitcham

HALLOWEEN NIGHT

It was finally October, moonlight sparkled through the night. Dad asked me if I wanted to celebrate Halloween by going somewhere scary. We chose to go to an abandoned hospital and go dress up as zombies...
When we arrived, Dad found a knife and played with it, then it landed on his head and he fell dead.
I felt a bit sleepy so I slept on those beds.
The next day, I saw Dad with no head! I turned around, a dark figure walked behind me. Dad was going to kill me so I ran far, far away...

Rayan Moussaif (10)
Gorringe Park Primary School, Mitcham

THE HAUNTED HOUSE

Tara woke in her bed after the worst nightmare and wanted to get some air so she went outside. She spotted a house and decided to go closer.

As she opened the door, she was scared as it was creaking so much it hurt her ears. The first thing she could see was a red knife in the kitchen. She screamed as loud as she could! As she slowly went upstairs, she could see a terrifying doll walking after her. She was horrified! She closed a door and went in; she saw a person nailed to the wall...

Julia Kalisz (10)
Gorringe Park Primary School, Mitcham

THE VAMPIRE

One scary night at 3am, the scariest witching hour, a huge, black cloud of a thunderstorm came. Suddenly, I heard a wicked laugh from behind the trees.

I went behind the trees and it was a vampire trying to spy on me! I walked through to see if it was a real vampire. He looked at me like he wanted to suck my blood!

I ran back to my house as fast as I could. The vampire kept on following me wherever I went. I tried to shut the door but he was too fast so he sucked my blood...

Vivian Doan (10)
Gorringe Park Primary School, Mitcham

THE NIGHT OF DESPAIR

On the 8th February, on a very gloomy day, there was a boy called Steve who ran and ran away. He faced towards north and found a spooky house. But the worst thing happened, it started to storm away! He ran to the graveyard, feeling all scared, but knocked at the door on the night of despair. Out came a zombie who jumped and scared Steve! But in that moment came a ghost to carry Steve away. Steve dropped from the ghost and skydived for his life, and landed in a grave. What a night!

Yassar Muhammad Farooq (10)
Gorringe Park Primary School, Mitcham

A ZOMBIE IN A SPOOKY FOREST

In the scary forest, there's an old graveyard and once a zombie came out of the grave. Some people came into the forest. There was a boy that was eleven years old. Luckily, he was with his friends but he was the craziest. They stopped talking and entered the forest. They saw something moving so they went closer. The zombie saw them and they ran and ran. They stopped. The zombie was heading their way and he captured them! They became zombies and they attacked other people.

Alan Lak (8)
Gorringe Park Primary School, Mitcham

BLOODY PUMPKIN PUPPY

One rainy and stormy day, there was a weird, special-looking tent. No one really went in there except the deadly, bloody pumpkin puppy. Next to the ugly tent, there was a hideous mansion that people lived in.
On Halloween night, the bloody pumpkin puppy came out. That was the only time he came out but the people who lived in the mansion, that was their pet.
Sixty years later, everyone wanted to see their pet, the bloody pumpkin puppy, but he wasn't answering...

Dominika Boraczynska (9)
Gorringe Park Primary School, Mitcham

THE HOUSE

On an early morning, a family were moving house. They took one last photo of their house. The daughter was the last person to see the photo. She noticed a creepy girl with a teddy, a photo and a Polaroid camera. Dad was about to close the door and saw the photo on the floor that he saw a second ago. He closed the door, got in the car and looked at the window. He saw the creepy girl waving. The car slowly rolled forward and crashed into the car in front... he died.

Kieran (11)
Gorringe Park Primary School, Mitcham

THE BLOODY HUMAN WEREWOLF

One night, a man called Michael Jackson went for a stroll. By the time he looked at the moon, his face went grey and inside his body, his heart was beating fast. He thought he was going to die! This was nothing new though, it always started at the face then slowly, the hair on his arms got longer and longer, his teeth got sharper and sharper until a drop of blood slowly dropped on his sharp tongue. He wanted one thing and one thing only - human flesh.

Taiyon Harper-Fuller (7)
Gorringe Park Primary School, Mitcham

LOCKED IN A BASEMENT

Four children, Stanley, Paige, Jake and Rachel, went down to the basement. Jake wasn't much of a speaker, that's why they didn't worry about him, but today they had to.

When they got down there, Jake was just daydreaming. They heard a scream and ran for the door but it was locked. Jake went to the corner to find some tools to open the door but after, they heard him scream.

After that day, they never went back there again...

Wilma Sanyanga (10)
Gorringe Park Primary School, Mitcham

THE MANSION NEWS AND THE GIRL

At 3am, witching hour, a huge cloud of thunder boomed and growled over the deadly landscape. In the depths of a dark and possessed mansion stood an abandoned cottage. A girl called Emily went to the mansion to see what was going on.
A few days later, news came that she was dead, but we didn't know because she never came out. No one knew who to believe, we needed to find out...

Bhavini Vimalan (9)
Gorringe Park Primary School, Mitcham

THE PICTURE

One day, there was a man called Jack, who moved into an old, abandoned house so he decided to take a picture on his Polaroid camera. As he took one, he saw a mysterious, shadowed figure, then he took a picture behind him. The mysterious figure was right there! The camera hit the ground with blood all over it and that was the end of Jack. Would someone dare take another picture?

Rio Cole (10)
Gorringe Park Primary School, Mitcham

THE EYEBALL CRUNCHER

One stormy night, there was a monster called Eyeball Cruncher. He was waiting for some children that always came on Halloween. They were nice and juicy! Eyeball Cruncher's mouth was full of blood from eating and drinking children from another village.

Then he heard footsteps, he loved eating children. He opened the door and *crunch!* The children were gone!

Annaliese St Louis (7)

Gorringe Park Primary School, Mitcham

THE MYSTERIOUS HOUSE

At 3am, the scariest hour, there was a haunted house that no one would go in. There was a boy named James and he went into the house... He saw a piano playing all by itself and he thought that a ghost was playing the piano. When he saw the piano playing by itself, all the other things were controlling themselves. He got scared and got out of the house!

Roman Miri (9)
Gorringe Park Primary School, Mitcham

THE SCARY FUNFAIR

At night, there was a funfair on. I asked my mum.

She said, "Okay, let's go!"

When we got there, there weren't many people around.

"Let's go to the mirror maze!" I said.

When we got in, I shouted, "Mum!" but she didn't reply. My sister and I tried to get out. Then all of the rides shut down and we didn't hear anyone talking. I heard a clown laughing. I didn't know which way it was coming from.

"Ha ha ha!"

"It's there, run! Quick!"

"He has got a shoe, ouch!"

"Just me, Dad! Did I scare you?"

"Yes!"

Hayden Terry (10)
Great Ballard School, Chichester

THE MYSTERIOUS CLASSROOM

In 2016, Ashley and Kate were in history. For some reason, they thought the teacher was transforming into a witch.

Ashley asked Kate, "Do you see that?"

"Yes," replied Kate. "Watch out!"

The books were flying everywhere. Everything went pitch-black. They heard gunfire and fires crackling.

"Kate!" shouted Ashley.

"Yes?" replied Kate.

It was smoky so they couldn't see. Suddenly, the light came back on.

"We must be in World War I!"

They looked over to the teacher, she was gone. Ashley hugged Kate but she went straight through her.

Ella Wakefield (9)

Great Ballard School, Chichester

THE ABANDONED HOUSE

I was there. A trail of blood led me to an abandoned house with blood-red curtains. I forced myself inside the wooden doors of the house and ran through the hallways and into a room with candles and a single deflated balloon. I heard whispers coming from behind the sofa but I didn't dare look. I ran upstairs and into another room.

I heard, "Surprise!" and saw all my friends. What were they doing here? Then everything became clear. The trail of blood was red paint and it was my Halloween-themed birthday party!

Olivia Cook (9)

Great Ballard School, Chichester

THE DEAD BUDDY

I opened the door and walked in.

My mum said, "Are you ready?"

I replied, "Let's go!"

We ran in and suddenly, it went very cold. I looked around. My mum had frozen! I jumped back and fell over. My friend was sitting on the sofa.

I said, "Hi, would you like a drink?"

She said, "Yes!"

I got her a drink. The queue was huge. It took forever. I took a plastic cup and gave it to her. It went straight through her hand and onto the cold floor...

Charlotte Hayesmore (10)
Great Ballard School, Chichester

THE CREEPY WALK

I entered the woods with my black Labrador, Carlou. As soon as I unclipped the lead, he ran off, chasing a rabbit. I was left alone.
Suddenly, darkness enveloped the woods. Although it wasn't cold, I could feel a shiver run down my spine. I could feel the goosebumps rising on the back of my neck. It felt as if someone was watching my every move. Could I feel someone's breath in my ear? What was making the twigs snap? Could I see someone's shadow?
"Oh, Carlou, it's only you!"

Lottie-Rose Best (9)
Great Ballard School, Chichester

GRANNY

I locked myself in the bathroom. Gran was going insane! She was so savage.

It all started weeks ago... I gave her a glass of water. She complained and wanted tea, I made a cup of tea. Then she asked me to get the gazelle out of the freezer, how weird is that? One week later, she said, "Gather the pride. Go kill a deer..."

Then the day came, she flipped. She was truly savage, her clothes ripped, she was hairy, scary and roary. Growls came at me. *Silence.* She glared at me and pounced...

"Arrghhh! Run!"

Daisy Amelia Mundy (10)
Heene CE Primary School, Worthing

THE HORROR HOUSE

Once, a half-lion, half-mouse creature crept fiercely through a haunted house.
I walked into the house. The door creaked open. I wandered around and saw another dark monster. I was screaming! It had beacon-red eyes and razor-sharp teeth. I immediately knew what to do. I tried to run with my books. This place was called The Horror House. The monster was called Scream!
I ran up the stairs. The stairs turned flat and I slid down!
After a wild goose chase, I and Scream came together. He said he was just saving me from the creature.

Aditya Vasisht (7)
Heene CE Primary School, Worthing

THE HALLWAY

It all started on the second floor, the darkest hallway in the hotel. When it is midnight, you can barely see the other person on the other side. The strange thing is that nobody books a room on that floor, but one day, Jonathan tried.

At midnight, he woke up but it wasn't on purpose. He walked into the hallway, then the next day, he went missing...

Police have been investigating this for years now. It started in 2001 and the floor has been unavailable since 2014. It's in London and the hotel is named Jewel Manor. Good luck!

Charlie James Fox (10)
Heene CE Primary School, Worthing

THE HELIUM BALLOON

There was an ordinary boy called Adab. Adab wanted to go to a meeting at 9.00. So off he went.

At the house where the meeting was, it was haunted. Adab slowly pushed the creaky door. Something jumped out - a vampire! Adab ran, the vampire chased him through the haunted house. Adab thought that in each room, a new vampire jumped out. Adab ran up, there he found a ladder. *Shall I go up? Yes!* He ended up in the attic. He found himself with King Vampire and some balloons.

"I will kill you!"

Adab escaped with a balloon.

Iona Sherwood (8)

Jessie Younghusband Primary School, Chichester

HOME ALONE

Mum and Dad had been due back ages ago and Sam was worrying. He was looking for them out of the window when suddenly, there was a piercing scream. Sam raced upstairs, Alice was crouched on the bed, breathing hard. Books were flying off the bookshelves! Before Sam could think, the lights flickered out. In an instant, they flickered back on. Just then, the doorbell rang. They rushed to the door, it was Mum and Dad, or was it? Their eyes were dead and lifeless, their skin was pale. Dad reached out a bony hand and smiled a chilling smile.

Isabelle Coton (8)

Jessie Younghusband Primary School, Chichester

SPOOKY

Bang! Crash! I felt wood splintering, falling on my face. I felt empty, not the sort of empty you would think. Empty, as in I felt like I'd forgotten something but I forgot what I'd forgotten. I looked around but all I could see was a faint outline of some stairs, then lights turned on and I saw a door so I stood up and dragged my soft hand along the rough wall.

I turned the door handle and out jumped a vampire, making me white with fear. I ran faster than sound and I closed the spooky door.

Noah Baverstock (8)

Jessie Younghusband Primary School, Chichester

FRIGHT NIGHT

I slipped. I fell. I fell into the lake. My heart was pounding. As I looked around, I could see a skeleton swimming after me. Suddenly, I started turning and sinking. I thought I was drowning! I realised it was a whirlpool. I got sucked in... I got teleported!
I was lying on a splintery floor. I was in an attic. Out of the corner of my eye, I saw a skeleton around the corner. I got up and... what was that noise?
It was just my alarm clock. It was a nightmare! Thank goodness for that!

Ava Lily Harman (9)
Jessie Younghusband Primary School, Chichester

THE HIDDEN CASTLE

Once, a little boy called Max was sent into the forest. Max went deeper and deeper into the forest until he saw a hidden castle. He went into the castle and it was dark and creepy. Max saw bats! When he went further into the hidden castle, he saw glowing red eyes, it was a vampire! Max was terrified! He ran and ran but could not find the way out. He was even more terrified! He got a sharp stick. He stabbed the vampire in the heart and found a family and lived happily ever after.

Daisy Dearing (8)

Jessie Younghusband Primary School, Chichester

CAPTURED

I was falling. When I hit the ground, I heard a crack. I thought I had broken a bone but I had no pain inside or outside. Then I saw it, a figure hammering away.

"Hello," I whispered.

It turned around and there was no face! I screamed. It covered my face and took me to a rank-smelling room.

That was six years ago now. I never thought writing would help but it did. Now my hand is getting cramp and the monster will be here soon. Why? Because I am a slave.

Rosa Brown (8)
Jessie Younghusband Primary School, Chichester

KNOCK, KNOCK WHO'S THERE?

I was sitting on the sofa. I heard a loud knocking on the door. I went to open it but when I got there, there was a giant figure in the window of the door. I didn't know what to do. Suddenly, it disappeared. I turned around and it was in the other window. *Slam!* It whacked the window.

"Let me in!" it bellowed.

It yanked the window open and took a box she had never seen before and ran away.

Olive Kus (8)

Jessie Younghusband Primary School, Chichester

THE BOAT TRIP

The Miller family decided to go on a family trip out on a boat.

"Are we all ready?" asked Mum.

"Yes!" shouted Meghan and her brother, they were so excited!

They got on the boat and started their journey.

Her little brother, Maison, shouted, "There are thunder clouds!"

They were going in the opposite direction, or so they thought...

After a while, they saw that the clouds were above them. Maison was scared so he went downstairs.

"Arghh!" he screamed.

There was a dead body there. Suddenly, a wave flipped the boat over...

Nikki Toth (10)
Meridian Primary School, Peacehaven

THE BLADE

The blade had done its job, Ivy was dead. Her wounded chest was cold and smothered in ruby-red blood. Fiona was the murderer. Fiona was also Ivy's friend...

That evening, Fiona went wandering in the treacherously gloomy forest and saw Ivy's ghost looming in the shadows. It was colourless yet the brightest thing Fiona had ever seen. Fiona slumped onto the ground, gazing up mindlessly at the ghost.

She died there and to this day, roses grow in a heart shape intertwined to represent their friendship. The thorns are sharp, showing their betrayal, scarlet roses for blood.

Mollie Haselup (9)
Meridian Primary School, Peacehaven

THE AFTERLIFE

When Dylan's death came, it was swift, swift as a racing horse. It wasted no time. One moment, he was in a forest, the next, in a dark, eerie realm of afterlife.

"Where am I?" whispered Dylan as he tried to feel his way.

Darkness swallowed light and glittered. He gave a mighty punch into the black galaxy and floated his hand back.

"You must be new," echoed a sinister voice.

Dylan started to panic. Salty sweat dripped down from the side of his face, his legs began to shake like jelly and his stomach clenched more than ever...

Marissa Hollie Palmer (10)
Meridian Primary School, Peacehaven

THE HAUNTED DOLL

One stormy night, Sophie sat wrapped up in her warm, fuzzy blanket whilst thinking about the mysterious doll lurking in her wardrobe. She had a strange temptation of throwing it out of the window. Her gut twisted at the idea of it. *What if it comes back to attack me or something?* Sophie suddenly heard a noise coming from inside the wooden wardrobe. She stood up and slowly approached it. Hand trembling, she opened it and the doll was gone. Sophie turned around and saw it on her bed. She had black eyes, blood running down her cheeks. Sophie screamed.

Michalina Fielek (10)
Meridian Primary School, Peacehaven

THE KNIFE

The girl with blonde hair dashed to the exit in the white mansion, which wasn't that white anymore because of blood stains that covered a quarter of the walls or more. She tripped on a wooden plank and fell over, her emerald eyes full of fear. She *knew* it was the end of life as a shady man approached her.

He smirked and secretly pulled out a shiny knife which was sharper than a butcher's one. Another stabbing was done. Another red drop to the bottle and another victim to be killed. The shining bottle was almost filled with blood...

Elizabeth Shalonina (9)
Meridian Primary School, Peacehaven

GRACIE'S GHOST

Gracie was going to spend her summer holiday at her grandmother's. She hadn't seen her since she was a baby. Grandmother showed Gracie her room, it was awful! She wished she was at home in her own bedroom. Gracie woke up in the middle of the night, saw a ghost. It led her to the past... She went back to sleep. When she woke, she was dressed as a scullery maid! Gracie was petrified, her heart was pounding! She felt like she wasn't awake. She was dead. Someone from the past stabbed her and that was how Gracie's life ended.

Anya Davis (9)
Meridian Primary School, Peacehaven

SPOOKY FRIENDS

I awoke in the middle of the first night in my new house. The air was cold and I could feel a presence. I peeped out from under the covers.
"Hello," whispered the girl at the end of my bed, "are you hungry?" she said, quietly.
"Who are you?" I asked, my heart beating wildly in my chest.
"I'm Sophie, come on, let's get some food."
As I walked to the kitchen, Sophie walked through the wall. I realised this was no ordinary house. I hoped we could be friends.

Ruby Roberts (10)
Meridian Primary School, Peacehaven

ANGEL

I moved into an abandoned house. Now it was getting murky outside so I went to bed.
I woke up and heard someone crying downstairs. I wanted to check it out but I was too anxious. I stayed under my cover.
After a few minutes, the crying stopped and someone was now laughing. Then it was coming up the stairs...
I dug myself under the cover. I then saw my doorknob turning! The door opened... it was a boy angel with red-hot devil eyes. It was floating like a ghost and had glowing chains. "Help!"

Luna Saulyte (10)
Meridian Primary School, Peacehaven

SPOOKY NOISE

It all started last night when Ellie couldn't get to sleep. She was looking up at her dolls and she heard a noise in the attic so she went to check it out. She didn't see anything. Suddenly, she heard a big bang in her room and then she ran into her room, leaving the attic door open. All of her dolls were all over the floor and her big doll named Bella was sitting on Ellie's bed, staring at her. She screamed and her mum ran to her and asked what was going on. Ellie stood there, silent...

Isabelle Raggett (10)
Meridian Primary School, Peacehaven

THE STORY OF CAMP BURCK

One night in Camp Burck, one girl called Aliza and one girl called Cristall were around a campfire telling scary stories but while they were so busy, they didn't know that the stories came true! One story came true, the story of the Camp Burck zombie. He roamed around at night, lurking through the darkness.
One night, a zombie walked around hunting for food. He banged on the girls' window violently as he crawled. The girls realised there was one way to escape: one person had to be bait...

Faith Vickery (9)
Meridian Primary School, Peacehaven

CAMILLA AND THE KIDNAPPER

Once, something extraordinary happened to me. I was in my bedroom relaxing when something alerted me. It was my phone which was in my school bag.

As I stood up, I walked to the other side of the bedroom but something grabbed me from behind. What was it? It looked like a creature. I could tell due to the wiry, messy hair that covered the thing's face and that's when I found myself in an unknown cave. The thing was a human that was very curious. It crept towards me curiously...

Lilly Knapikova (9)
Meridian Primary School, Peacehaven

THE MASK SHOP

One day my friends and I were outside a mask shop. we decided to go in and take a look inside. once we were in the shop we noticed a door with a sign saying *NO ENTRY!*
we turned and saw a figure. He said nothing so we continued into the mysterious room. There were loads of cool masks. We tried the masks on but we couldn't take them off. I pulled and pulled until I woke up at home in my bed. It was all a dream!

Olivia Julie Coughtrey (9)
Meridian Primary School, Peacehaven

DON'T GO TO THE DUCK POND AT MIDNIGHT

Have you ever walked past a duck pond and heard ducks quacking? Is it really harmless quacking or something more sinister? Well, I can tell you a story about the night my journey home took me past our village pond.

It was a dark and moonless night, difficult to see. As I neared the pond, the ducks started their chorus of cackling. I thought that the sound was like evil laughter or maybe they just tell each other jokes. It was then I learnt the truth about ducks as I saw the red eyes and razor-sharp teeth... I ran!

Abby Tittle (11)
Peasmarsh CE Primary School, Peasmarsh

THE OMINOUS FIGURE

I was playing in the woods and went back for dinner. I was playing on my PS4 till eleven o'clock at night but then I realised I'd left my jumper in the woods. I ran upstairs, grabbed my torch and walked to the woods.

When I got there, I went in and saw my jumper by the abandoned shed. I went and grabbed it but that's when it happened, a flash of thunder revealed an ominous figure in the darkness. It started running towards me with bloodstained hands. Would I live?

Nial Wilde (10)

Peasmarsh CE Primary School, Peasmarsh

13 KAMMASTER ROAD

Many years ago in Manchester, there was a house, 13 Kammaster Road. It had been abandoned for centuries and the legend tells us every thousand years on Halloween night, children have been stolen and put in the house. None have ever returned...

This Halloween is a thousand years after the last, so Trevor doesn't know what's coming for him.

Meet Trevor, who loves Halloween, but this might be his last.

"Quick! Quick!" shouted Trevor. "This is the last house!"

Trevor walked in, the door was already open. He felt like something was wrong. Then someone grabbed him aggressively...

Oliver Skinner (9)
St Joseph's Catholic Primary School, Haywards Heath

THE TALE OF TOMMY TERROR

Tommy sprinted through the dark, foggy woods. He slowed to catch his breath and saw messages written on the trees in thick, scarlet blood: *Keep running!* He ran like his life depended on it. Panting, he cleared the forest. He forced himself to turn. Standing there was a life-sized doll, a knife in its bloodied hand. "Boo," it whispered, an insane smile spreading across its porcelain face.

Lifting the bloodstained knife, it aimed for Tommy's petrified face. Tommy screamed and sat bolt upright in bed. A dream? Then he saw it, scrawled on his mirror in vermillion blood: *Boo!*

Joshua Foy (10)
St Joseph's Catholic Primary School, Haywards Heath

THE SPOOKY SCHOOL DAY!

As the bell rang, parents all left, the children were alone. A dark cloud towered over the school! Shivers skated down the children's spines as they realised the horror. All the teachers had morphed into giants and monsters! A nightmare had begun!

Miss Brown stormed out of her classroom and screamed, "No playtime at all today!"

Some children fell to the floor in agony and pain!

Suddenly, Mrs Walker bellowed, "Get up! Extra homework for all of you!"

Children cried and clung onto each other out of fear, as yet another day at St Joseph's School had started!

Emma Grace Rochford (10)

St Joseph's Catholic Primary School, Haywards Heath

MY SOPHIA DOLL

Late that night, when I found my macabre Sophia doll weeping at the kitchen table, I asked, "Umm... Sophie, what's wrong?" shaking in fear.

She turned her head and showed me the bloody knife in her hand and mumbled, "No matter what I do, you won't stay alive!"

I sneaked back, keeping a really close eye on her to see what she was up to next. I turned around to see her holding the knife right to my face. Slowly, she walked forward as if she was going to swipe the knife right through my neck. Blood covered the walls.

Brooke Bashford-Dickens (10)
St Joseph's Catholic Primary School, Haywards Heath

THE GHOSTS OF THE PIPES

This is a story that will make your brain burst, your knees knock and bogies squirt out of your nose, so if you don't want this to happen, I recommend you shut this book immediately! There were once four children, nothing scary about that, right? Wrong. Here's the catchy bit, they were ghosts of unfortunate kids who clogged up the pipes to grab their victims. That tragic day, it happened. Something beyond belief. New pipes were laid at a school nearby and on Monday, all the children vanished, dead or alive, no one ever knew!

Daisy Belle Stoodley Leppard (10)
St Joseph's Catholic Primary School, Haywards Heath

UNDER THE BED

It was a stormy night and Molly was whimpering in her bed. She just had the worst nightmare. She had it every night and always hated it. It was about a monster under a bed who came out at night.

This particular night, she didn't get to sleep. Her eyes stayed open, her hair was blowing in the wind, then she suddenly heard something. It was a monster! She screamed till her jaws couldn't open. The monster was blue with horns on his head. He looked scary but he said something that made him seem friendly...
"Be my friend?"

Emily Daisy Hilton (9)
St Joseph's Catholic Primary School, Haywards Heath

THE PYLONS - KATIE'S NIGHTMARE

It began when I was in the car, in a deep sleep. I started to hear a thunderous noise coming down the motorway. In a flash, I was awake. I silently peered out of the window and saw these pylons ripping out of the ground. I was wondering what was happening. They were stomping on cars and treading on people. They seemed to be marching towards the seaside! Everyone thought that they would be killed by these spark-spewing, electrifying creatures but all along, they just wanted to meet the other pylons below the splashing sea. What a spooky day!

Katie Rochford (8)
St Joseph's Catholic Primary School, Haywards Heath

WHY?

My best friend was called Molly. One day, after arguing, she told me I wouldn't see her again because she was moving away. I was distraught!

Yesterday, something unsettling happened. I was in the mall bathroom, plaiting my hair in front of the mirror, when I saw the shape of a familiar girl in a pure white blouse with wavy, ginger hair. She was crying, apologising, but when I turned, she wasn't there.

Later, I discovered that Molly had died after arguing with me. It was then that I recognised the girl's face. Molly, why?

Aglaïa Carvalho-Dubost (10)

St Joseph's Catholic Primary School, Haywards Heath

THE HAUNTED HALLOWEEN PARTY

The air turned black around me, light flickering and blood dripping from my skin. It was Halloween night. Me and my friend went to a Halloween party!

When we arrived, nobody was there. We were confused but thought we were just early. My friend went to the bathroom which left me alone.

An hour passed and my friend didn't come back. I crouched to go see her but saw her lying dead with a bloody mouth. I was petrified! I knew I was next... I sprinted, heading to the door but it was locked. I turned around in disbelief...

Chelsy Mae Dupiano (10)
St Joseph's Catholic Primary School, Haywards Heath

THE SHAPE

One dark night, you are walking along the road, only a dim flashlight is showing you the way. Suddenly, a silhouette catches your eye in front of you and as you approach, you hear faint cries. You want to look at it but you're afraid.

As you walk by it, you see its long arms and legs. He's as pale as a full moon on Hallows' Eve. The noise stops. You turn around, your eyes locked. Frightened, you run but as you stop, you turn back. Nothing is there. Relieved, you pivot around and there he is, in your face...

Alex Ladd (9)
St Joseph's Catholic Primary School, Haywards Heath

WHAT A MISTAKE!

Pumpkins are actually quite sophisticated vegetables, despite being carved and baked into pies. They're the best in the whole vegetable patch. Except for Poe, he was a pumpkin and not a very good pumpkin. Not only was Poe bad, but he was also dumb too! So guess what he dressed up as for Halloween? A pumpkin! Yes, a pumpkin.

Poe trundled off at an alarming rate. He knocked at the first door. The lady peered at her doorstep. A great big orange pumpkin sat there. The woman was a great baker...

Elsie Tibble (9)

St Joseph's Catholic Primary School, Haywards Heath

SEARCHING IN SPOOKY VOICES

Hi, my name is Annabelle, I'm fifteen. My parents have gone shopping so I'm exploring the house today! Although, I'm getting worried, they've been out for hours and my childminder hasn't arrived! Wait, I can hear something coming from the attic. A screeching noise. I wonder if it's the cat? No, she's at the vet's. Oh, who is it?

As I'm creeping up the stairs, the noise becomes louder, screeching, screaming, shadows everywhere around me! Suddenly, I trip... but there are no boxes on the attic stairs. Oh, it's a foot!

"Annabelle?"

It's the... it's the childminder...

Genevieve McArdell (10)
St Joseph's Catholic Primary School, Redhill

WHAT'S THAT SHADOW?

"Goodnight!" shouted Margaret.

It was Halloween and Margaret didn't want any nightmares that night. She didn't fall asleep until midnight...

She felt herself fall from a cliff onto solid, hard ground. She couldn't see anything. Then she started to see some blue, some green, some red. Margaret looked around and a dark shadow appeared. Margaret's eyes popped open - she couldn't believe what happened. She sat up and saw the same shadow from her dream. It started to come to her. She hid her fear. As the shadow came closer, it scratched her face with its slender finger...

Leigh Steadman (10)
St Joseph's Catholic Primary School, Redhill

THE FIGURE IN THE DARKNESS

As Emily climbed up the ladder, she was thinking about what would be up there. Probably mice or bats, but ever since she had heard that knocking, she was eager to find out what it was.

When she finally made it to the attic, the knocking started louder than ever. Emily immediately tried to find where it was coming from but when she turned the corner, she saw a tall, dark figure standing a metre away.

"Who are you?" she asked, trembling.

There was no reply. Next thing Emily knew, all she saw was black. Nobody ever saw Emily again.

Florence Moore (9)

St Joseph's Catholic Primary School, Redhill

WELLIES

Running out of school, Clara headed into the cold, dark evening. Her horse, Monty, needed attention.

Whilst greeting Monty, a fog started to roll in across the damp field. She had a strange feeling trickling up her spine. Someone was watching her. Carrying on with her jobs, Clara felt uneasy. A twig snapping caught her attention. A howling voice echoed across the vast field. In a trance, Clara walked towards the voice. A pair of red wellies. Following them towards the hedgerow, Clara crawled through the brambles and into a dark abyss.

Isla Mehta (9)
St Joseph's Catholic Primary School, Redhill

THE DEVIL'S HIDE OUT

One ordinary day, a little boy's family were moving to a new house since Jason, the little boy, had just joined a new primary school. One Saturday morning, Jason was looking around the house to see what was where, when he spotted an attic door. Sadly, it was padlocked. Jason was desperate to find out what was up there so he looked around on the carpet for a key. It was there! He slowly unlocked the attic and went up and saw a black devil just standing there in the corner. "My attic is a devil's hideout!"

Isaac Blackburn (9)
St Joseph's Catholic Primary School, Redhill

THE VAMPIRE WHO WAS AFRAID OF THE DARK

My name is Milia and I am a vampire. Let me tell you a secret, I'm afraid of the dark!
It's Halloween tonight and Mum and Dad are trick or treating with Tilly. I sit in my room, reading. Suddenly, there is a noise from outside. I grab my torch and take a look around the door. Out in the corridor, there's a dark shape. *Plink!* My torch goes out. Just then, I realise that it's a werewolf! I back under the painting of Count Vudu. The werewolf looks above me, then runs off. I look up and smile, scary!

Sophie Pither (9)
St Joseph's Catholic Primary School, Redhill

FOOTSTEPS

I could no longer ignore the scuttling coming from above my head. It was driving me insane! I unlocked the creaky loft hatch, climbed the ladder and peered into the darkness... The light of my torch caught the shimmers of cobwebs, but they were made by no modern-day spider. Eight glowing blood-red eyes, the size of saucers, peered at me through the darkness. My torch then flickered and died, leaving me with only one source of light, the eyes, but where had they gone? I felt a hairy leg creep over my shoulder...

Charlie Rocco Knap (9)
St Joseph's Catholic Primary School, Redhill

THE GREY STRICKEN NIGHT

As I stumbled up the dragon's tail, I was blinded by a monstrous castle which had turrets that looked like the fingertips of a withered witch. Suddenly, a lightning bolt struck me down. Unable to move my body, paralysed with fear, I shouted up to Heaven to help me. There was nothing but an echo... A queue full of questions filled my head. Would someone hear my sorrowful cry? Would my body come to the rescue? Had I simply met my fate?

Joshua Jupp (10)
St Joseph's Catholic Primary School, Redhill

THE MYSTERIOUS SCHOOL

There was a girl called Danielle. She had brown, curly hair. She found out that she was stuck in the brand new school!

"Hello?" shouted Danielle.

She went down the clean, shiny stairs but then she got pushed down them. She could hear keys jingling... her arm! It was broken! She got scared, then she fainted!

When she woke up, she said, "Where am I?"

She went back upstairs and went into an office. It was all black. Then she found out it was her scary, horrible teacher!

Mollie Ann Bradley (8)
Stafford Junior School, Eastbourne

THE ONE-EYED MONSTER AND ME!

It all started on an ordinary morning when a brown, furry monster with one eye came up to me. It smelt like a wet dog! It was the Sweet Snatcher! I didn't have any candy. Then all of a sudden, a furry hand shot out at me and grabbed me!

After that, I woke up in some sort of rotten cave but it looked like my den I made last summer. I kept trying to escape but it was too hard.

Finally, I realised that I could kick him so I did and ran all the way home!

Charlotte Smeeton (7)
Stafford Junior School, Eastbourne

THE CHILD'S LAST SCREAM!

Late Friday night, Charlotte wandered up to her friend's house and as she went in, something rushed behind her.

"Are you okay?" asked Amelia.

"Yes, I'm okay."

Charlotte was at Amelia's for five hours.

As she left, something rushed past her again.

"Who are you?"

She turned to wave goodbye.

As she was walking down the path, she saw a shadow again.

"Who are you?"

"I'm Nigeni and I'm here to get you, Charlotte!"

"Go away!" She ran and ran into a bag and was captured and it ran with her. Amelia saw it and she ran to help.

Natasha Zoe Downes (9)
The Globe Primary Academy, Lancing

THE HOSPITAL

On a normal evening at the dinner table, Sidney was waiting for his dinner when his mum's phone rang. It was Sidney's grandad phoning.

He whispered, "Come over to the hospital right now, I can hear things screaming and screeching!"

They ran out of the house.

Sidney got there. It was deadly silent. They looked in all the wards, nobody was there. They looked in his grandad's ward. There were lots of monsters.

They all looked around and shouted, "You two are dead!"

The two humans screamed and they disappeared instantly. They ran back to their house.

"We're safe now!"

Nathaniel Dene (9)
The Globe Primary Academy, Lancing

SEVEN NIGHTS AT SCHOOL

One gloomy night, Jamie and Fraser went to the park and saw an abandoned school with blood over it.

"Shall we go in?" Jamie whispered.

"No! Why would you want to go in there?"

"I didn't, I just wondered if you wanted to go in."

"Okay, if you really wanted to go in, but you have to go in first!" said Fraser.

"Okay fine!"

They entered and saw a ghost called Ragnarok. Then they blinked and he was gone...

"Where did he go?" said Jamie.

"Dunno," said Fraser.

Just then, somebody came up behind them.

"Arghh!"

Harry Waddup (9)
The Globe Primary Academy, Lancing

BIO ZOMBIE

In the seas of a blood-swollen battlefield sailed a battleship that shot 300 pounds of chemicals, from three long barrels, onto the enemy in order to end all wars, but another just began... Zombies!

A freakshow released in all its fury. Within a flash, zombies speedily swept through Europe. In the city of Berlin, everything was suppressed and there were few survivors hiding in old air raid shelters.

Soon, hope came! America dropped nuclear bombs on every country that the zombies had entered and infected. Humans needed to protect themselves from threats like this. War isn't good!

Zachary Manser (9)
The Globe Primary Academy, Lancing

PLEASE KEEP ARMS CROSSED AND HEAD DOWN AT ALL TIMES

It was dark, spooky and horrible when Layla opened the creaky, rusted gate. There was a flapping, wet Halloween sign at the entrance. In enormous letters, it spelt: *You will regret this!* Layla managed to cleverly encourage her friends to join her.

As they stepped into the park, Layla spotted a helter-skelter in the foggy corner of the park. "Come on, scaredy-cats!" called Layla.

She quickly grabbed a sack and confidently slid down with a happy scream. Her friends stared down the horrific slide. Nothing. She didn't come out the other side... just some bones...

Yolanda Isabel Thomas Negro (10)
The Globe Primary Academy, Lancing

THE HAUNTED CASTLE

The world spun as I fell. I landed on something hard. A door creaked open. I stood up and looked down and with horror, I saw a skeleton. It began to walk towards me. I screamed and ran for my life.

"Uhh!"

The sound was so faint, I thought I'd imagined it. Suddenly, a stooped figure stepped out of the shadows.

"Uhhh!"

A *zombie!* I picked up a rusty sword off the floor, just as three more zombies jumped out of the shadows. They advanced.

I woke up, sweating all over. Suddenly, I heard, "Uhhh!"

They were in my room!

Charlie Nettlefold (9)
The Globe Primary Academy, Lancing

THE BLOB FROM NOWHERE!

Suddenly, a zombie mutant bursts out of an atomic factory and drags its legs through the creepy, abandoned house. It drifts through the nailed-up door.

Meanwhile, a colossal radioactive blob drifts through the basement walls. The zombie stands still, then grows to the size of fifty skyscrapers and is as wide as thirty-six school buses. Weirdly, Bloby shrinks fifty times smaller. The blob latches on the mutant zombie's head and the zombie gets bigger and bigger until it explodes with baby zombies.

They were the last monsters ever seen. Well, at least I hoped they were...

Jack David Standen (10)
The Globe Primary Academy, Lancing

THE DROP

One stormy night, a girl called Charlie heard banging in the attic. She just thought it could be the bucket that caught the drip-drop in the roof. Of course, she didn't go up because Charlie just couldn't risk being late out with her friends. She went simply to go and say goodbye.
"Bye, Mum, see you later!"
"Okay, see you later!"
Soon, she heard the drip-drop again. She had to check it out. Off she went...
"Arghh! The monster!"
Pounce! The monster was now on Charlie.
"Arghh! Please help, help me!"

Indiana Bazeley (10)
The Globe Primary Academy, Lancing

THE PETRIFYING PIZZERIA

Whilst I was having a delicious Hawaiian pizza, there was a kid's show featuring a robot named Freddy Fazbear. Strangely, the lights went out and everybody around me vanished without a trace. Suddenly, the robot wasn't on the stage. I ventured down the hallway but I heard robotic movements behind me. I turned around, nothing there. I was horrified to see a message saying: 'You're dead!'
Then a screeching shriek came out of nowhere. Speedily, I began to sprint, only hearing my heart pounding. All I wanted was a nice time. Freddy appeared. I was for it!

Jorge Sexton (10)
The Globe Primary Academy, Lancing

THE VAMPIRE TEACHER

It was a dark, cold evening when a little girl walked into the dark streets. She walked up the hill and into a building with ivy covering it. The little girl wondered why there were tables, pencils, rulers and chairs in it? The little girl saw a dark shadow and blood dripping.
She screamed, "Who is there?"
Someone turned. It was a vampire! She looked around her. There were millions of people lying with vampire teeth marks!
"Mr Evans, what did you do to them?"
"I needed them, just like I need you!"
"Noo!"

Olivia Marsh (9)
The Globe Primary Academy, Lancing

THE LAST NIGHT

"Hello?" I shouted.

"Who is it?" a voice came back saying. "I am going to get you!"

I jumped. "Who is it?" I trembled.

"It is Gooey Ghost!"

I started walking into the darkness.

Then Gooey Ghost shouted, "Boo!"

I jumped. As I got closer, the ghost's voice got louder. I took one last step. There was complete silence. I did not know where I was, what I said or what my name was. It was pure silence until I heard a noise behind me. When I looked back, I saw Gooey the ghost...

Megan Clarke (10)

The Globe Primary Academy, Lancing

THE CRAZY HALLOWEEN

It was Halloween night, Lizzie knocked on the door of the creepy playhouse.
A man opened the door and said, "Come through!" in a scary voice.
She went through and opened a door.
"Arghh!"
She was getting wrapped up in mummy bandages and duct tape around her mouth.
She thought it was a joke and laughed.
Suddenly, all the people dressed up were real.
They had green eyes and made scary sounds.
Bang! Boom! Guts went everywhere!
The door fell open. It was Dad! He tried to free her but the bandages stayed on!

Libby Bedford (9)
The Globe Primary Academy, Lancing

ABANDONED HOSPITALS AREN'T FUN

One gloomy night, a young boy was walking along a pathway and he saw an abandoned hospital. He just *had* to go in! As he was, he heard a voice...

It was saying, "Go away!"

He still went in anyway.

A gruesome monster called Mackley was saying, "Go away or I will rip you apart!"

When he went in, a large monster said, "I warned you!"

The monster, Mackley, was breaking him away and last minute, he ripped the boy in half, piece by piece, until the boy was dead. Then he ran as fast as he could.

Elliot Braiden (10)

The Globe Primary Academy, Lancing

TRICK OR TREAT NIGHTMARE

One gloomy, dark night, when the clock struck ten, a girl called Olivia went trick or treating with her friends, Lily and Evie. Then they stumbled across a haunted house on a creepy hill. The girls all desperately wanted to enter the house so they went up to the ghostly house and knocked on the uninviting door. The door opened but nobody was behind it. Lily and Evie were terrified and ran down the hill, however, Olivia wasn't scared.

Out of nowhere, Olivia heard a chilling scream. She turned around but Lily and Evie were long gone...

Olivia Lockwood (10)
The Globe Primary Academy, Lancing

THE TELEPORTING GIRL

After school, I went to my usual park. I went alone and there was nobody there. Surprisingly, a girl appeared out of nowhere. This was off as I didn't hear the gate open.

"Hi," my voice quivered.

Strangely, she didn't say anything back. Suddenly, she disappeared but then reappeared on the slide. I felt a chill go down my spine. As she disappeared again, I felt like I should run but I couldn't. I was frozen to the ground! Then she appeared next to me, grabbed my arm and we disappeared into thin air...

Layla Pelton (10)
The Globe Primary Academy, Lancing

THE NO-NAMED BOY

"Arghhh!" he screeched.

He was pacing up and down a corridor that seemed very unfamiliar. Panting with every step, he opened a door on the far left of the corridor. This boy didn't have a name, his parents died before they could give him one. Looking through the door he had just opened, a mysterious fog was travelling towards him at quite some pace. Suddenly, he heard the door slam shut behind him! Too afraid to look back, he jumped under some covers of the bed in the room.

He was back in his room...

Sidney Ager (10)

The Globe Primary Academy, Lancing

THE NIGHT OF THE LIVING MASK

One morning, Jason and his best friend said they wanted to find a creepy, abandoned haunted house.

That night, they went together to find a creepy, abandoned haunted house. By this time, it was midnight. They found the house they were looking for. There were lots of walking masks! Dylan and Jason stood there in shock! They slowly walked past the walking masks to the door of the abandoned haunted house. Jason and Dylan were really scared!

They went up the creaky stairs to the guest room. In there, was the master mask...

Oliver Snuggs-Lee (9)
The Globe Primary Academy, Lancing

THE SPOOKY, SCARY SCHOOL

I woke up in shock and fear. Frightened, I looked around. At that moment, I knew I was at school. However, there was bright red blood scattered on the floor. I was horrified! Quickly, I sprinted over to the door and walked along the corridors. I saw a person with no eyeballs! Suddenly, I turned away. Then I looked back. He was a doll! I heard whispers whilst walking towards the door to escape. It didn't open so I knew I wasn't alone... I sprinted.
"Arghh!"
I tripped over and the person was behind me!

Mimi Raynsford (10)

The Globe Primary Academy, Lancing

THE PHANTOM BOY

In broad daylight, in a scary forest, there was a church just standing there. A boy called Bronson walked up to the church.
Suddenly... *Kabam! Crash! Broom!* The church doors opened and a rainbow, eight-legged phantom flew out and chopped a head off. It grew another one. The head that was chopped off exploded!
Then night struck. A zombie apocalypse came to Bronson and threw him up to the phantom. The phantom ate Bronson, then turned into the little boy. The phantom went back to Bronson's town...

Chloe Brisley (9)
The Globe Primary Academy, Lancing

THE DINNER LADY STRIKES AGAIN

Olly walked up to the dinner lady. Thinking she was friendly, he asked her for the beef soup. She whispered, "Of course, my lovely, anything for you!"

She gave him the soup. Strangely, it was moving... He went to sit with his friends but then everyone dropped dead, landing on the floor. Olly turned to the dinner lady and she was gone too! The school bell rang but where were the teachers? The only thing he could see were the empty classrooms. He walked outside, everything had disappeared...

Evie Hilton (10)

The Globe Primary Academy, Lancing

THE CHURCH OF DEATH

One bright Sunday, I was strolling to my local church when suddenly, I saw a sign: *Zombie Infestation, Do Not Enter!*
Scarily, a man with his eye filled with blood whispered in my ear, "This is all your fault!"
I sprinted to my house but Mum wasn't there. I noticed the undersides of my feet were wet. Mum entered. Without warning, she walked up to me and tried to bite me. For safety, I ran into the church, however, there were zombies everywhere. I ran away but I tripped...

Ella Croome (9)
The Globe Primary Academy, Lancing

THE ZOMBIE FRIEND

As the clock struck twelve, I ran out of my
house to my friend's den in the forest of gloom.
The day before, we planned to meet there.
As I arrived at the entrance, I felt a tingling
shiver down my spine,
Moments before I set foot in the forest, I heard
a blood-curdling scream. I knew it was her. I
ran as fast as I could, even though I knew it
was dangerous. Just then, I felt heavy
breathing down my cold neck and I knew it was
the end of me. Olivia had turned into the
zombie cheerleader...

Bethany Hall (10)
The Globe Primary Academy, Lancing

GHOST

It was a foggy morning, Kelly was eating her dinner. When she finished, she moved on quickly. She went outside. Suddenly, Kelly saw a boy on the road. He didn't move a muscle. A blue car was on its way.

She screamed, "Move!"

Somehow, the car went right through him and he vanished! In shock, she sat by a bench where she noticed a poster that said: *Missing Boy.*

That was the boy she just saw! Suddenly, she saw a shadow before hearing a scream. She ran so fast!

Ruby Heywood (10)
The Globe Primary Academy, Lancing

THE MYSTERIOUS SCHOOL

The teacher, who was wearing torn clothes, walked down a creepy, derelict hall into a diner filled with zombie kids, apart from one child.
In one second, someone bellowed, "I'm hungry for brains right now!"
The kid fell to the floor in shock! The creepy teacher stared at the girl and spoke again.
"Hungry for brains, must eat brains!"
The teacher spoke to the kid and she woke up. Everything disappeared into plain sight... but her head felt strangely empty.

Chloe Douglass (10)
The Globe Primary Academy, Lancing

THE HAUNTED FAMILY

The kids went downstairs for breakfast and there was something there, they couldn't quite see it though, so they went and looked and it pulled them into a soundproof box. It was a king monster and it bit the kids' necks! They screamed but no one heard. They turned into monsters and went upstairs and bit their parents' necks. They turned into monsters too! Then they went to the baby's room. The baby turned into a monster with no eyes and no tummy, you could see through him!

Faye Walls (9)

The Globe Primary Academy, Lancing

THE BOY AND THE CLOWN

It was 12pm at night. I was home alone so I went to shut my blinds. When I did that, at the corner of my eye, I saw a red balloon and holding it was a clown. I was devastated but then I shut my blinds. When I was shutting them, I had a tap on my shoulder. Sweat ran down my forehead. I thought to myself, *it can't be the clown, he's outside!* I turned around, it felt like I was coughing blood.
"Arghh!" I screamed.
I shut my eyes and the clown was gone...

Matthew Floate (10)
The Globe Primary Academy, Lancing

THE HORRIBLE HOSPITAL

Last night, I was walking down my road when I heard a scream from the abandoned hospital. Then the lights in the streets went out. I was left in darkness! Suddenly, I heard footsteps closing in on me. Then I saw it, a ten-foot skeleton covered in blood! It was pushing me into the hospital!
When I reached the spooky haunted black door, I saw why it was called Abandoned. Bodies were all over the floor and blood was everywhere but it wasn't from the hospital, it was from me!

Adam Hacker (9)
The Globe Primary Academy, Lancing

THE GHOST FRIEND

One bright sunny day, a girl called Lauren and her friend, Liam, played outside their houses. Liam wasn't paying attention where he was going and he ran into a vicious dog who kept attacking him!
Soon after, he was taken to hospital. Liam was eating his food when Lauren visits him every day until the chefs created a fire in the kitchen. Liam could not escape.
It was his funeral when he was buried and Lauren went to his grave every day.
One day, she saw him...

Erin Atkinson (10)
The Globe Primary Academy, Lancing

FATAL FOOTBALLERS

One night, the bright yellow glowing moon shone over scary Stamford Bridge. Chill-sea Ghosts were about to play a blood-curdling charity game against Scaregulls. The stadium stood silent as the two terror teams hovered out onto the pitch to play ghostball, football for ghosts.

After ten terrible minutes, the keeper got kicked in the shins. He fell unconscious for a while but then blew up into bits. All of the lights went out, every fan sank into the ground but I did not...

Lewis Sharman (10)
The Globe Primary Academy, Lancing

THE TOWER OF MARY I

As the clock struck 3am, a monstrous guard heard a noise upstairs and cracking from a fire. He went up the creaky stairs and he heard something walking down the hall, knocking all the knights in shining armour down as the fire continued rolling through the floorboards. Someone shouted, "It's the return of Mary!" The noise grabbed the guard and took him into a room full of fire. It threw him into the fire and exclaimed, "It's time to die!"

Liam Floate (10)
The Globe Primary Academy, Lancing

THE DEATH OF ME

One late night, I woke to a ping from my phone. I read the text and put on some comfy clothes. Since both doors were locked, I jumped out my bedroom window. As I walked away from my house, I ambled into an abandoned building. Near me, I saw a man with a name badge: *Benny The Killer Clown.* Oh no! I ran towards the door until it shut on me! The last thing I knew, I had been knocked out.
I then awoke, red stuff dripping from me. I was not alive. I was dead...

Grace Harris (10)
The Globe Primary Academy, Lancing

THE SCARECROW AND HIS GAME

One evening, a little girl called Kara was supposed to go to a party but she decided to go out with her friends, so she did. She and her friends went past a creepy house with a scary scarecrow. So they went to it. They went so close that the scarecrow came alive at the sound of a bang! They screamed and almost died. The scarecrow's eyes turned black. They were all running and the scarecrow turned them into zombies and made its own gang! "Arghh!"

Jorja-Carol Harris (9)
The Globe Primary Academy, Lancing

THE HAUNTED MANSION

I woke up at midnight and heard a scary sound. I was frightened! I was trying to find Mimi. Maybe *she* screamed.

After a while, she was behind me.

When I looked back again, she was gone. Then I saw a doll but it disappeared. Then I saw Mimi, so as quick as a flash, I ran outside. Mimi was lying on the floor with blood all around her! Then I ran back in the house into my bed. I went under my cover and went to sleep.

Then, I got eaten...

Demi Leigh Leggett (9)
The Globe Primary Academy, Lancing

THE MYSTERIOUS DINER

Olivia walked into a diner and looked around and thought, *this must be decorated as a sixteenth-century diner.* She walked up to the counter and asked the lady with red hair, "Is this a new diner?"

"No," the lady replied.

"I'd better go now!"

Olivia walked off, then she looked back and saw a knife floating towards her. All of a sudden, she fell dramatically to the floor and everything was gone...

Lily Green (10)
The Globe Primary Academy, Lancing

IN THE CUPBOARD

It was a dark and gloomy day. A girl called Rose was home alone when she heard strange voices coming from the cupboard. She went to investigate. She slowly opened the creaky cupboard door when a vampire jumped at her... She screamed and ran away.
Before long, she heard another terrifying scream. Instantly, she ran back to her parents. *Too late.* Rose got her phone and called for help... *It's just a dream*, she told herself.

Lily Hollingdale (9)
The Globe Primary Academy, Lancing

FUNHOUSE NIGHTMARE

After school, on a warm, sunny day, Juliet and I went to the local funfair. As a joke, we decided to go to the funhouse and scare people! I looked down a maze of glittering, glossy mirrors and saw myself in all of them. Suddenly, I heard a young girl's ear-piercing, deafening scream. I turned around and Juliet was gone. I looked in the shiny mirror behind me but couldn't see myself. I could only see poor Juliet on the floor...

Isla Riley (9)
The Globe Primary Academy, Lancing

THE LITTLE GIRL IN THE WOODS WITH HER DOG

She was camping in the woods. She saw a shadow in the moonlight. Her dog turned into a horrible zombie dog. The girl was terrified. Her dog ran! She saw red blood on the bus. Creepy eyes were in the big bush. She saw a clown standing, watching her. Her body was shaking. She almost couldn't talk. She was terrified of the horrible clown! His teeth were black and one of his eyes was black. She ran and ran, the clown grabbed her...

Brooke Dixon (9)

The Globe Primary Academy, Lancing

IN THE ATTIC

Once upon a time, a small boy called Bob was home alone but then he heard a noise coming from the attic, so he got a ladder and a flashlight on his phone and made his way up the stairs.

When he got there, the noises stopped. There were two people planning something. He went into the dark loft and saw a dark figure. Suddenly, he found himself awake in a hospital bed. It was just a dream, until he looked in the corner...

Ebonii Humphrey (9)
The Globe Primary Academy, Lancing

THE GIRL IN THE WOODS

Once there was a girl that was lost in the woods. She heard a blood-curdling scream. She saw a lady.

The lady said, "Don't just stand there, run!"

She ran. The lady followed her back to her house.

The next morning, she realised she was living with a ghost! She tried to run away. She was stopped at the door. She backed away and turned around only to be stopped!

"Arghh!"

Kara Price (9)

The Globe Primary Academy, Lancing

THE MARIO GAME

One week ago, I got a Mario game. I decided to play it but Mario had bleeding eyes and a hole in his chest. I couldn't open my door.

Then I fell asleep. I walked through a corridor in my dream and saw Mario get killed.

I woke up seeing my mum dead and my nose was bleeding. I burnt the game and called for help but they told me my mum did not make it. I've been having nightmares ever since.

Darsh Khadka (9)
The Globe Primary Academy, Lancing

GRAVENHILL

The bus was late, it was dark and nobody was in sight. Eventually, it arrived.

"Where to?" the driver said.

"Gravenhill."

I looked behind me and screamed. A weak hand clutched me.

"Don't go to Gravenhill," it said in a hoarse whisper.

The bus stopped. I got off and the bus disappeared quickly. I heard a long groan, I was standing on a grave, a mouldy hand coming out of it. I screamed... Creatures were coming out of the forest. Something put its hands around my neck.

"A clown!" I gasped.

It laughed wickedly. I knew this was it...

Eve Baker (10)
The Towers Convent School, Upper Beeding

MY NAME IS CINDY

Three kids found a parting in the woods. A house appeared! A high-pitched noise made their ears throb, but they could not stop themselves walking towards it. The door slowly opened, creaking. Strangely, they could not turn back. They followed the deafening noise. They reached the attic. A figure appeared, dragging its feet across the floor as it slowly hovered, its emerald eyes staring into their soul.

"My name is Cindy, come play with me!" she sang.

The kids let out an almighty scream. They ran as fast as they could home. They never forgot that day!

Amelia Birse (9)
The Towers Convent School, Upper Beeding

THE SPOOKY NIGHT

It was a stormy night and I was sleeping in my bed.

Suddenly, *bang!* was what I heard under my bed...

"Ugh!" I said. "It's just my mind playing tricks on me."

I went back to sleep.

Rustle! I heard it again but this time, there was whining and scratching.

"Okay," I said, and I jumped out of my warm bed.

It was very chilly. So I looked under my bed and saw nothing, then I looked again and saw my cheeky kitten.

"Oh you silly boy, Elvis!"

He hopped into my warm bed with me.

Kitty Rayner (9)

The Towers Convent School, Upper Beeding

A SPOOKY STORY

I was sitting at my kitchen table, planning my spooky story. There would be ferocious animals, their eyes flashing like they were watching me. I looked up, the sky had grown dark.

"Wow!"

The whole sky lit up with a flash of lightning. *I'll include that in my story*, I thought. Then a door banged shut. All went black. I found myself in my own spooky story!

Eyes were glaring at me from every direction, my heart was beating like crazy. Slowly, I reached out my hand but then something clamped over my mouth. This was the end of me.

Sophia Nicholls (9)
The Towers Convent School, Upper Beeding

LIGHTNING CLOSE

We walked up to the door of a creepy house. It was storming loudly, there was a full moon. I knocked and knocked, there was no answer. A strange creaking noise made Sophie jump. The door opened, there was no one there.
"Arghhh!"
A doll came running towards us.
"Hello," said the doll quietly.
"Awooo!" howled a wolf.
There was a flash of lightning.
"Luna, be quiet!" shouted a haunting voice.
Shadows lurked around... something was there.
"Sophie, let's get out!" I screamed.
Crack! Crack! The doll crumbled to bits. We ran out and the house demolished.

Megan Robins (9)
West Rise Junior School, Eastbourne

FREAKHOUSE

"Where is that phone?" I asked Mum.

"Oh, just in the cellar," replied Mum, "be careful!"

I soon found myself walking down the creaky steps of the cellar.

Bam!

What was that noise? I thought to myself. I was absolutely petrified! *Bam!* I heard the noise again.

I'm really not liking this, I thought.

"Arghh!" I screamed in fear.

I totally jumped out of my skin. It, it was a doll! Not just any doll, but one that could move and talk. It started to walk towards me.

"Arghh!"

The doll's eyes were mere slits.

"Oh my! Arrghh!"

Mitch Morgan (9)

West Rise Junior School, Eastbourne

THE CREEPY MOONLIT NIGHT

Lightning struck outside my bedroom window. I was in my cold bedroom listening to the rain patter on the ground. Suddenly, I heard a voice.

"Hello?" I stammered. "Anybody there?"

I shuddered, then I heard constant screaming.

"Arghh!" shouted the voice.

My doll started moving in the darkness. Suddenly, the lights began to flicker. The tap started running and the radio turned on. There was something under my bed.

"Help me!" I screamed.

I knew it was a bad idea but I looked under the bed... there was somebody there. I tried to move but I was frozen in fear.

Amelia Gurr (9)

West Rise Junior School, Eastbourne

HAUNTED STORIES

Where am I? Is this a haunted house?
I reached for the door but it didn't budge. The creaky floorboard suddenly started to collapse in the dark room.
"What was that noise?"
I walked towards it. The door opened. I saw two dolls. I screamed internally. I froze on the spot, gulping. I heard something.
"Rebecca," whispered someone.
I looked back at the door but the dolls weren't there anymore. I heard screaming.
"Arghh!"
Then a door slammed. I wanted to run but I couldn't, I couldn't get out.

Stefania Turcu (10)
West Rise Junior School, Eastbourne

CHILDHOOD NIGHTMARES

I was just walking up the stairs when I heard it, a tiny voice coming from my room. I also heard muffled voices occurring from my radio, saying weird things like: 'Man killed by doll'.

The stairs creaked as I hurried up them. I was so creeped out that it felt like I had literally jumped out of my skin. I had just opened my bedroom door when a flash of lightning struck close to my house. I saw something move just out of the corner of my eye.

"Arghh!" I screamed.

I saw it scramble up the window...

Eve Isobel Van Der Geyten (10)

West Rise Junior School, Eastbourne

HAUNTED HORROR HOUSE

One thundering night, I heard a bang. My bedroom door creaked open. I sprung out of my warm bed onto the floorboards. Suddenly, the lights turned off. Through the hallway, a ten-metre long shadow stretched from under the door. Just after I blinked, arms wrapped around me. My head shook at the sound of a bang. I couldn't see anything!
"Where am I?" I asked myself.
There was a bright glow in the basement. There was a man with a statue head, which fell off. Then I realised that it was my dad, surprising me.

Louie Emo (9)
West Rise Junior School, Eastbourne

YoungWriters®
Est. 1991

YOUNG WRITERS
INFORMATION

We hope you have enjoyed reading this book – and that you will continue to in the coming years.

If you're a young writer who enjoys reading and creative writing, or the parent of an enthusiastic poet or story writer, do visit our website **www.youngwriters.co.uk**. Here you will find free competitions, workshops and games, as well as recommended reads, a poetry glossary and our blog. There's lots to keep budding writers motivated to write!

If you would like to order further copies of this book, or any of our other titles, then please give us a call or order via your online account.

Young Writers
Remus House
Coltsfoot Drive
Peterborough
PE2 9BF
(01733) 890066
info@youngwriters.co.uk

Join in the conversation!
Tips, news, giveaways and much more!

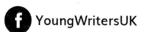 YoungWritersUK    @YoungWritersCW